Ariel

A When Doves Cry Book, Volume 1

Amy McCorkle and Melissa Goodman

Published by Amy McCorkle, 2023.

ARIEL

First edition. May 23, 2023.

Copyright © 2023 Amy McCorkle and Melissa Goodman.

ISBN: 979-8223053712

Written by Amy McCorkle and Melissa Goodman.

Chapter 1

In the beginning, they were made. No one rested on the seventh day. Ariel and Adriana Stuart were six years old. This year their family gathered to celebrate the holidays. Their father Gerald, normally stoic and unemotional, was tender and kind to them on occasions like these.

The twins were as different as night and day. Ariel, a concert pianist prodigy garnered the spotlight. Adriana, forever in the shadow of Ariel was desperate for her father's attention.

Their mother Isabel commanded the room as usual. She was the epitome of a social butterfly and the most beautiful woman in the room. She successfully charmed the foot soldiers of Gerald's "organizational family as she sipped the finest wine with one hand while lavishing affection on Gerald with the other.

Two bodyguards stood on the periphery surveying the room. Gerald kissed his wife, and motioned to the guards.

"My darling, must you attend to business? It's Christmas Eve."

"I'll only be a moment."

A lean dark-haired man sat down next to Ariel.

"Hi," he said sipping a brandy.

Ariel ignored him as she continued to play.

His blue eyes danced as she mesmerized him with her talent. He set his drink on the piano and began to play the harmony to her original arrangement.

She smiled and continued to play.

"Matthew," Gerald called. "My office."

Matthew sighed and picked up his glass, draining it. "Sorry my angel, duty calls." He stepped away. Ariel's bodyguard, Stone Ramsey, had watched the whole interaction. His expression was impassive.

Beale, Adriana's bodyguard whispered to Stone, "That was interesting."

Gerald and Matthew soon approached. Gerald cleared his throat and looked toward Stone. "Nothing goes unnoticed in my home. Does it Stone?"

"No Sir."

"Into the office, shall we?"

THE FOUR OF THEM SAT in silence. Gerald looked at Matthew, his lawyer, he was young and hungry, but far from stupid. Stone was the major muscle, street smart and loyal to his warlord and his princess. Beale on the other hand was dangerous. He was loyal, but he eventually would have his own organization.

This meeting was one of those things he did not mention to his wife Isabel.

Gerald and Isabel together only had the twins. Gerald had an illegitimate son with Isabel's sister Kate. Their son, Zachary wasn't eligible to inherit the lion's share of the power. He would eventually make a move for it though. Gerald needed his daughters and empire protected.

Guardianship decisions were in the process as to who would raise the twins in the event of his and Isabel's death. He loved his partner Leo like a brother. Leo had proven recently that he too, might like to rule his empire.

Leo covertly began his coup. He sowed seeds of discord with Zach. Gerald noticed that Leo got along with Adriana, but did not care for Ariel. Fortunately, neither twin trusted or liked Leo. This was as much of a relief as it was a worry to Gerald.

He'd always imagined Matthew as their guardian and Beale as the heir of the empire. This would leave Stone to guard the girls. This exchange between Matthew and Stone worried him.

He wanted a different life for Ariel than being the one to rule at Beale's side. She seemed built for another kind of life.

Adriana on the hand, was lean and hungry and playfully obsessed with Beale Alastair. This concerned Isabel.

"Matthew I have drawn up the papers we've discussed. In the event of my and Isabel's death, guardianship goes to you. I know Adriana has a cute crush on you, but it's Ariel, when she comes of age that I feel needs to be matched with someone strong. Not someone who will cheat on her. I won't have it."

Stone's fingers gripped onto the arms of his chair.

Matthew noticed, because he also clutched his glass of Brandy.

Beale was listening intently. He knew his choices were between the sharp as a tack lawyer, and his silent savage best friend.

"And as for Adriana?" Beale asked coolly.

"This life isn't for her either. But she may choose her match."

Matthew interjected, "Do you think that's wise?"

"I agree," chimed the usually silent Stone.

"There is a mole inside my organization. Matthew, find them. And when you do, report back to me."

A series of loud bangs rang out. Women screamed. The startled men turned as the door caved in and a masked individual opened fire. Stone and Beale hit the ground. Matthew dove for Gerald. It was too late. Gerald laid in a pool of his own blood. The rest bled profusely. Matthew touched his chest soaked with blood. Darkness came for him as Beale and Stone started firing. Matthew's only thoughts were of the charming twins, the musical angel in Ariel, and the intelligent power of Adriana. But it didn't matter. The pain was too much and darkness greeted him.

Chapter 2

Stone charged into the living room. He surveyed the carnage. Isabel, Ira, Sam, Jeff - all dead. His heart pounded - the girls. Where were the girls? Where were Ariel and Adriana? They must've hidden or been taken. Who would take them? His mind went straight to Leo. He would take Adriana. But Ari? He detested her. Leo was the kind of cold-blooded bastard who would definitely murder a kid.

Some foot soldiers had limits. Hungry ones like Leo didn't. Stone's stomach twisted.

He stooped down next to Isabel and closed her eyelids. "Sorry Izzy."

He stood up. Looked around again. Something was off about the scene. Kate and Zach should be among the dead. They were missing as well.

A sickening feeling settled into a knot. Beale came up behind him, Stone whirled around, his gun aimed.

"Whoa!" Beale shouted.

"Kate and Zach aren't among the dead."

"The twins?"

"I can't decide if that's the good news or terrifying news, they're not in here either."

"Did you happen to notice if Matthew survived the ambush in the office?"

"No. Right now I don't care."

"If he didn't, Leo is the defacto guardian through their Aunt Kate."

"Fuck!"

"We have to find them first."

A mournful scream came from the office. Both men turned and made a beeline for the office.

ARIEL STUMBLED INTO the office, her white and silver dress soaked in blood. She was quickly losing consciousness. "Addy," she whispered.

Adriana didn't hear her. She was too traumatized. Leo had tried to hurt her. She ran when she saw him coming again. She went to the one person who could fix it. Too late, Gerald was on his back, his eyes open and vacant. The light gone in his eyes. He was dead.

Adriana shook him. More blood oozed from her injuries. She was alive, but her daddy was dead.

Ariel had been shot. She was aware her dad was beyond saving. She looked down at the floor. Matthew was slumped against the wall in the sitting position. His shirt soaked with blood. Tears gathered in her eyes.

"Addy..."

"Ari," Adriana gasped.

Ariel fell against Matthew. Matthew's eyes opened and widened. Somewhere from deep within he gathered Ariel in his arms.

"We're going to survive this. All of us."

Adriana looked up. Beale appeared in the doorway. Stone spoke. "That's smoke I smell."

Beale lifted Adriana. Stone helped Matthew as Ariel clung to him.

"She's been shot," Matthew rasped.

The sound of glass breaking and flames crackling neared.

"The papers..." Matthew rasped, "the custody papers."

Beale looked around for the envelope.

"It's there," Adriana said.

Beale reached to the floor.

"Move!" Stone shouted.

Adrenaline fueled them as they ran from the house. The fire engines arrived as Ariel blacked out and Adriana watched her childhood burn to the ground.

Stone looked to Matthew as sirens announced the incoming ambulance.

"You understand what has to be done now?" Stone asked.

"Yes," Matthew responded.

"Are you prepared?" Asked Stone

"Of course not. But I'm ready. And I'll need yours and Beale's assistance," said Matthew.

Beale turned to Matthew.

"You may be their guardian, but the empire is mine."

Adriana crawled out of Beale's arms and went to Ariel. She looked at Matthew and back to Beale. She'd always seen the way Stone and Matthew positioned themselves where she and Ari were concerned. She knew they cared about her. But they were really invested in Ariel.

She focused on Beale. Beale loved both of them. Beale wasn't her father. But he was built for this world just like she was. It was at his side she belonged. She was only six, but she knew her future.

"Ari," she whispered. "We are only beholden to one another. So, fight. But only for me. Only ever for me.

Chapter 3

Matthew woke with a start. He looked to his right. Ariel slept in the hospital bed next to his. Stone slept in the chair covered in a sheet.

"Stone."

Stone jolted awake. He looked from Ariel to Matthew.

"Is she going to be okay?"

"She sustained several gunshot wounds. It's a miracle she's alive. The next 72 hours are paramount."

Matthew attempted to get up. Ariel stirred.

"Matty...no..." she murmured. "Wake-up...please wake-up..."

Her vulnerability crushed him. He had to protect her. And even though he and Stone didn't trust one another, they were going to have to work together to keep the twins safe. There was only one way he could think of to keep Ariel safe: send her out on tour.

Adriana was attached to Beale. Almost to the point of obsession.

Stone had a colorful past as a gigolo. However, where Ariel was concerned, he was a saint. Beale on the other hand was the definition of a wild man.

He hated the idea of separating the twins. Boarding school might be the only solution for Adriana. God knows she would hate him. For that matter, Ariel too. But their safety until they were of age was paramount.

"Stone, I think I have the answer to the twins safety."

"I'm listening."

"Ariel is a prodigy."

"You're thinking of a national tour."

"To begin with."

"And Adriana?"

"Boarding school."

Stone scoffed at him. "Do you think either of them will react well to that idea?"

"Let them hate me. I only care that they are safe They need to survive their childhood and adolescence."

"And who will be guarding them?"

"You will tour with Ariel."

"Yes."

"She's six."

"She idolizes you."

"But she trusts you."

"And Beale?"

"Beale was Gerald's annointed one. Right now, he's too wild to take care of a child. Let him run Gerald's empire. You can hand pick one of our European assets to watch over her."

"Adriana will hate you."

"Let her."

"So will Ariel."

"Let them both hate me. As long as their breathing I've fulfilled my duty as their guardian."

"Stone?" Ariel said opening her eyes. She looked to Matthew, then to Stone. Stone rolled his stool to the bed and took her hand.

"I'm here."

"Where's Addy?"

"Beale's with her in the examining room."

"Is Matty okay?"

Matthew crawled out of bed and sat next to her, "I'm right here."

She started to cry.

Stone pushed away from the bed, and said, "I'll be right outside."

Matthew held her hand. He dreaded the moment he would have to send her away. He would comfort her and do his best to do as Isabel and Gerald would have done until then.

ADRIANA WAS QUIET IN the aftermath of the rape kit being done. Beale entered the room. He looked at the doctor. The doctor's grave look said everything. "She refuses to say who did this."

"Why don't you leave me alone with her?"

Adriana watched the doctor reluctantly leave. Once she and Beale were alone she held her hand out to him.

He took it and sat with her.

"Who did this to you?"

"Beale, you know who did this to me."

Beale tried to hide the rage bubbling up in his chest. He didn't want to frighten Adriana. She'd been through enough this evening.

"I'll kill him."

"I'm counting on it."

"Did he shoot Ariel too?"

"Yes."

"Then you know Zachary and Kate were left untouched."

Adriana nodded, tears coming to her eyes. "I'm scared."

"He will never touch you either of you again."

"I know. Daddy trusted our safety to you and Stone."

"Matthew is your guardian."

"No."

"Yes, Addybelle."

"I said no!"

He touched her cheek. "He may be your guardian, but you are *mi familia."

"Promise me you won't ever forget me."

"I promise."

Adriana grabbed onto Beale. She knew they belonged together, but she was just a child. She would have to bide her time, but she would never forget him. And he would have to earn her love all over again.

*my family

Chapter 4

Ariel would be nineteen soon.

She hated touring and everything about it. She always had. She always would. A little wind-up doll trotted out to perform.

The only real friend she had was Scott. He was a brilliant violinist. A prodigy who was destined for greatness and completely normal in every way. They were the toast of the music intelligencia. Scott adored her. Ariel knew all she would have to do was crook her little finger and he'd be hers forever.

It could never be. His mother abhorred their friendship. Ariel was untouchable. Every man wanted to either own her as a trophy wife, or leverage her for power. She wanted more. She desired to love and be loved in return without her scandalous past intruding on that.

Christmas loomed. She hated this time of year. And even though Addy was in Europe, they always made an effort to spend the holidays together. Matthew may have fumbled his way through their guardianship, but he had been careful with their inheritance, and did his best to guide them.

Ariel sat at her hotel desk, she had been composing a musical score as a gift for Stone and Matthew called The Mighty Sword and the Elegant Orator. She hadn't been able to get past the first movement. Earlier events in the evening had left a sour taste in her mouth. First, Adriana had met someone who fascinated her, some guy by the name of Frankie Galloway.

Every year Matthew had brought them home, well, their new home to celebrate together with Beale, Stone, and himself. They were an unconventional family at best. Though the holidays were an exceptionally sad time of year for them, it was oddly a time when her loneliness lessened.

She loved the theater, but she hesitated to go.

There had been a confrontation at the concert earlier with Scott's mother. She cringed just thinking about it.

"No son of mine is going to be seen with a slut's daughter and a criminal's offspring. "Why don't you go fuck your way to the top with that savage gorilla?"

Scott had just stood there as she rambled on about her hack playing skills, and how her shyster of a guardian bought her way into polite society.

Tears came to her eyes. She had said nothing. But Stone had taught her a few things about violence and appropriate times to use it. Maybe it was the time of year, or the nasty things she said. Maybe it was the venom and condescension in her voice. Ariel snapped.

Ariel roared and went to punch her in the throat. Stone stopped her. *"Come on, the high society cunt isn't worth it."*

The blood had pounded in her ears. She barely heard him. Stone placed a gentle hand on her shoulder.

"What did you call me?"

Stone gave her a look that put a stop to any more insults. Scott's mother backed away pulling her son along with her.

Ariel collapsed. Stone caught her and carried her out of there.

Tears streamed down her face. The once legible music smeared. The notes became blotches. No longer could she discern the notes she had written. She screamed and wrenched Scott's necklace from her neck. The chain broke and beads flew.

Stone barreled through the door. Barefoot and bare chested in blue jeans, gun drawn. The necklace struck his face. He set the gun down and shut the adjoining door.

Stoic, he stood there. Stone looked every inch the silent savage.

"I can't do this anymore."

Still, he didn't move.

"I just want to die."

His face betrayed nothing. Ariel could see his heart breaking for her in his eyes. There was something else, like he was restraining himself, and it was taking everything in him to do it.

"I hate this time of year."

"I know you do," he said his voice rumbling deep in his chest.

Ariel wiped her tears and cried again. "I just want someone I can trust in my life. Someone I can love and who can love me. None of this too weak to stand up to your mother bullshit."

"Scott's an ass. He says he loves you, but he has no spine. You deserve better," he said sharply.

Ariel cried harder. She felt alone. It cut deep. She slid to the ground and curled into a ball. "I don't belong here. I don't belong in polite society. Just pull the trigger now."

Stone dropped to his knees. He laid down beside her and pulled her into his arms. "I love you," he whispered into her ear. He tilted Ariel's chin upward and turned Ariel to face him.

"Teach me," she said.

He searched Ariel's face. "No."

"Please. One day you won't be here. And I will be alone."

He touched her cheek. "Promise me you won't turn into a monster like me."

"You're not a monster. You're the only one who understands me."

He growled and buried his face in her neck.

"Stone, I love you."

His lips brushed against hers and they kissed. She no longer felt alone.

Chapter 5

Stone watched Ariel as she slept. How long had she felt this way? He stroked her arm and ran his fingers through her hair.

He knew it was wrong to take her innocence like he did. But she was no longer a child. Ariel had grown into a striking beauty. With long, strawberry blonde hair and emerald-green eyes. When she played the piano, sometimes she would sing; it was like angels whispering in his ear.

There was a quiet pain to Ariel though. One that Leo and his faction had instilled in her when they took her family from her. Usually Christmas was hard, but when their odd little family was together, it made things a little easier for Ariel and her sister.

As he lay with her here in the quiet of the London night, he knew it was only a temporary fix. That her loneliness would return. The darkness would continue to haunt her.

There was only one person who truly made her happy, and that was Adriana, and maybe Matthew.

Beale was someone she looked to as a father figure. Matthew she related to on a much a different level. They were like besties when they were together. Their closeness made him jealous.

So, he held back. Over the last year he had kept his feelings in check. Watching helplessly as Scott clumsily made a play for her. Painfully watching in silence as she struggled with her celebrity status when all she wanted was to fade into the background.

Last night Scott's mother triggered her. Scott showed what a sniveling excuse of a man he was. She was spiraling downward; she asked him to end her life.

It became apparent she needed him. And he couldn't restrain himself anymore. He gave into what he was feeling. So did she and it had been better than anything he could have imagined.

Her eyes opened. She smiled. "Stone..."

"I'm here," he said softly.

She kissed him. "I've wanted this for so long."

This startled him.

"I thought you wanted Scott. I kept my distance because I thought you wanted normal."

"I realized last night I would never have normal."

"So, you settled for me?" he chuckled.

"No. I thought you weren't interested in me."

"You're everything to me. You have been for a long time."

He rolled her to her back and gently pushed inside of her. Her back arched and their eyes met. Her gasp confirmed it.

She placed her hands on his back and they came together in a frenzy. Of lust, love, and longing. Her body shook at his touch. They trembled as they came down from their long-denied ache and passion.

When they were quiet again, Stone felt her tears. Then heard her sobs.

"What is it, Ariel?"

"Nothing."

"It must mean something."

"Anytime I care about something, I lose it. I lost Scott as a friend. I lost Mom and Dad and my brothers. I'm losing Addy, Matthew is going to be so mad at us he won't be my friend anymore."

He wiped her tears away. "Sh, sh sh sh. Scott was a spineless piece of shit. Adriana is struggling and needs to sort some things out. As for Matthew, he's your best friend. He isn't going anywhere."

"I want my Christmas."

"Then you'll have your Christmas."

"Promise?"

"I promise."

He showered her face with kisses. He got out of bed.

"What are you doing?"

He stood in front of the window and looked down. Paparazzi swarmed. Shit. The incident last night was going to be in the papers and all over the internet. Matthew would be angry and place the blame on him.

He didn't prevent it. That it had landed on the front page. Ariel had been hurt by it and would continue to be hurt by it.

Stone couldn't say that he could blame Matthew. Matthew hated sloppy work where Ariel was concerned. The fact that they had fallen in bed together. Ariel was right, he wasn't going to be happy about that either. Anything that had the potential to hurt her was to be avoided.

When you loved someone, as much as he did, but didn't want to admit it. Ariel was right about love. She had lost big when it came right down to it.

"We have to leave."

"Why?"

"Last night is in the papers."

"Oh."

"But fuck them. I'm going to give you that Christmas you asked for."

She smiled at him and got out of bed. "I'm going to shower."

She walked to the bathroom. Stone followed her.

Chapter 6

Matthew was furious. Things like this were not supposed to happen. Publicity at Christmas time only dredged up the past in nasty ways. He had planned a faith-filled and inspirational event for the girls. It always felt a little forced this time of year. He had been right the twins would be angry all those years ago. He just hadn't counted on Adriana's rage, or Ariel's suicidal, self-destructive tendencies becoming problems.

Adriana at eighteen was sophisticated, rage-filled, and figuring out who she was. His phone call to Stone that morning included a debriefing of how close to the edge Ariel was.

He had done what he was supposed to do. Matthew placed them in therapy. Adriana and Ariel both had strategies to successfully defeat the therapists' good intentions. Adriana ran circles around them with her intelligence. Ariel was passive. She stared through them. The therapist could see the empty sadness and the walls go up at the same time.

When she did let you into those spaces, it could rip your heart out. He had sat with her in those spaces.

She had sat with him in his.

They had become close.

When Matthew had seen the front page of the New York Times, he had realized something. He didn't just love Ariel. Over the last year he'd crossed that line. Even though he and Stone had discussed it at length falling for Ariel was something he couldn't do.

"Matthew!" He heard her shout.

She was running. His heart skipped a beat. He stepped out into the hallway. She leapt in his arms and they squeezed tight.

"Oh, how I've missed you," he said. "We need to talk. I've planned something very special-,"

She looked over her shoulder and he watched her face light up in a way that broke his heart and he felt light die in him. He forced the smile to stay in place. His eyes met Stone's.

"Matthew, before you-,"

"Matthew I've missed you too. I have so much to tell you. But you first."

"Oh, I convinced your sister to come home."

She wrapped her arms around him and squeezed. "You are the best. You always know how to give me the best Christmas presents."

He and Stone locked territorial gazes.

"I have a delicious lunch set up on the terrace for us. We can discuss this latest incident then."

"You're not mad are you?"

"Of course, not darling. Now go," he whispered in her ear and kissed her chastely on the cheek.

Ariel looked to Stone and back to Matthew. She pulled free and said, "Play nice."

Ariel picked up her suitcase and headed towards her room.

Matthew turned to Stone. "How'd it happen?"

Stone said nothing.

"I asked you a question, I expect you to answer it."

"She was devastated. She asked me to assassinate her. I guess we were feeling things neither of us were aware of. We love each other and don't regret it."

"All the lectures. All the conversations. And you do what you told me not to do."

"I'm her bodyguard. You were her guardian. Different line."

Matthew said, "Pick up Adriana from the airport. Have the limo pick up Beale."

"I see. All I can say is don't fucking take it out on her."

"I wouldn't dream of it."

Stone turned and left. When he turned around Ariel was standing in the hallway. She took a half step forward.

"I didn't know."

"It's okay darling."

He smiled, but she knew him as no other. Tears filled her eyes and she raced away. He walked out onto the terrace. Candles lit. Food laid out. A tree up and decorated with special gifts that Matthew had known would touch her heart. Adriana would be there to help facilitate Ariel's rebirth and joy of the season.

All he had accomplished was to hurt her and reinforce in her mind Christmas brought nothing but pain. He couldn't leave it like this.

He followed her. Listened as the door slammed. Once at her door he knocked. "Ariel, can we talk?"

Only silence greeted his ears. He turned the knob and entered the room. She stood at the window.

"I fucking hate Christmas. All I feel is pain. The moment I feel any relief, and think, maybe I feel joy. I find out I'm causing you pain. I don't want that." She turned and faced him.

"You're not causing me pain. You could never cause me pain. Stone called ahead and asked me to set up something special just for the two of you."

"You're lying."

"Sometimes to avoid pain, we choose to believe a harmless lie."

It's not harmless if it puts a hole in your heart. You're my best friend. I want you to find love."

"I will."

"As my best friend, be honest with me."

"I created a private celebration."

Teardrops fell.

"Because you love me?"

"I've always loved you. I've only recently come to realize I am hopelessly in love with you."

Ariel walked up to him and took his hand. "Take me to the terrace."

Matthew realized this could only end in one of two ways. He or Stone would die. A fight was brewing. He knew neither felt like giving an inch.

Chapter 7

Nothing was going to happen on that terrace. Matthew had screwed Ariel's life up enough. He could tell that much when she balked at the entrance.

"I can't do this. I've made a commitment to Stone. I love him."

She released his hand as if she had burned him.

"What do you mean?"

"I almost died over there. I wanted to die. I was convinced, am still convinced life isn't worth living. Stone convinced me otherwise. I'm sorry. I'm sorry, I just can't."

Ariel tried to walk away. He grabbed her hand and squeezed. Her heart began to pound.

She ran from him. As fast as she could, as hard as she could. She needed her sister. She needed someone to sort out these conflicting emotions. She loved Stone. She had always felt they were inevitable. But with Matthew, he had always been there. A shelter from the storms of life. Stone was her physical shield whereas Matthew had been her emotional one.

Addy hated them both. She had never gotten over her life and security stolen away in an instant.

Ariel had gotten to retain Stone, and frequent trips home to see Matthew. He had become her best friend and confidant. When had things changed for him? Or for her that matter?

Matthew and Stone were her world. She was in an impossible position. To claim one, she would lose the other. Maybe she was selfish, or maybe she was just weak. They each spoke to a different need in her.

She didn't want to step away from Stone. So, as much as her heart had cracked open when Matthew had declared his love for her, the terrace and the potential it held had to remain closed until she could clear her head.

She made it to her room and ran out to the balcony. She gripped the railing taking deep breaths and counting to ten.

"I love Stone. I love Stone. I. Love. Matthew."

"Ari? What are you doing?"

"Trying to clear my head and stop a train wreck."

Adriana stepped up next to her. "I heard. You know I can't stand either one of them."

"I think that's the one thing I don't like about you."

"Listen, those men only care about one thing. How you get them up an organizational ladder."

"I almost killed myself in London, Addy."

"Stone filled me in. Did you have to sleep with him?"

"I don't know if I had to, but it made me forget the pain for a little while. Stone may be a brute, but he was quite tender with me."

"Do you love him?"

"I said that I loved him."

"Did he say it back?"

"He said it first."

"When did he say it?"

"When we were having sex."

"And you?"

"The same."

"And I know all about Matthew's terrace plans. What can I say, lame-o."

"I love the way you approve of my choices."

"I just want you to be happy, safe and loved. Really loved Ari. And men from this world don't know how to do it."

"Is this the point where we talk about Beale?"

"Beale doesn't give a fuck about me. There's nothing to discuss. You on the other hand, have two grown men making goo goo eyes at you."

Tears came to Ariel's eyes, a lump to her throat and she forced a painful laugh out of her body.

Adriana touched her hand.

"You want to jump, don't you?"

Ariel nodded. Tears hitting her sister's hand.

"They've put you in a position you're ill-equipped to handle."

"People think I'm so mature."

"When it comes to matters of the heart, I will say I have more experience."

Ariel thought about Stone's body moving with hers dissipating the pain. She thought about Matthew and the way he went out of his way to try and make her love Christmas again.

She associated Christmas with death. Matthew's grand gesture any other time would have won her over. Right now, she was consumed with suicidal ideation. Not even her sister could wrench her free from it.

"I can't deal with this." She stared vacantly ahead and seemed to leave the present day.

Adriana knew that look. Sometimes Ari took trips to the past. The only one with the magic touch in that regard was Matthew. Stone hated him for it.

Ariel sank to her knees and gripped the bars. "Don't die Matty. Don't die."

Adriana didn't like Matthew, but when Ari slipped into this state she became unpredictable. She could as easily slip away into a catatonic state as launch over the railing.

She couldn't leave her alone.

"Matthew!"

MATTHEW WAS SITTING on the terrace when Adriana's shouts for help. It took a split second for him to race through the corridor, the foyer, bound up the stairs and burst through the door.

Ariel was on the floor, her knees pulled to her chest rocking back and forth, tears ran down her cheeks. "Matty don't die. Matty don't die."

Matthew got down on the floor. He wiped her tears and enveloped her in his embrace.

"I'm not going to die Ariel."

"So much blood. So much blood."

"It's alright. The bad men are gone."

She wailed as she curled her fingers around his collar. Matthew pressed his cheek against her temple. He was so protective of her. Her need for him drew them together. But if she wanted Stone, he would have to swallow how he felt and rise above.

So smart, so talented, so compassionate. He didn't deserve her. It didn't stop him from wanting her.

Adriana intruded on their world. "Don't force her to choose. Step back and let her figure it out. I told Stone the same thing. She not equipped to make such a hard decision fast."

"I won't force her to choose. I won't abandon her either."

"You suck, I don't like you, I don't even think you're worthy of her. But, I know she loves you both. I wish Scott wouldn't have been a simpering, spineless, ass. On paper they would have been a match."

Ariel wept until she fell asleep. The pain of this world slipped away.

Chapter 8

Matthew watched her sleep from the doorway.

Something in her had finally snapped. Ariel had always had a fragility about her. Even though she seemed to have her shit together from the outside she was vulnerable to how the outside world perceived her.

"Remember what Adriana said."

Matthew turned to face Stone.

"You shouldn't be here."

"Exactly."

Stone had always been an immovable force who had given up a chance at ruling Gerald's organization to protect those girls. Stone and Beale were still as thick as fucking thieves. Their worlds had diverged, Beale building his own empire.

Now he and Stone were fighting over Ariel. He'd suspected it would come to it.

"I need to know that she's okay," Stone admitted.

Matthew said, "She had to be sedated. If you have to go in there, don't wake her."

"I am with her on tour. I have watched her wither on the vine. I lived through that night with you and her too. I watch her perform every night. I hear her cry herself to sleep every night. I can't fucking stand it. She's coming apart, and all you did was confuse her. You caused the flashback. You, not me. You understand that?

"It doesn't matter who caused it."

"If you actually believe that then you're more of a bastard than I thought."

Matthew was tired. He knew both he and Stone were at fault. That fragility that drew him to Ariel was the same thing that made Stone hopelessly soft for her.

Maybe the declaration of love was more impetuous than what his personality called for. Maybe Stone was right. Maybe he had triggered her flashback.

"We both chose to exist in this world. That makes us both bastards."

"When it comes to this family I am unquestioning in my loyalty. Especially where Ariel is concerned."

"Some counsel you are. You persuade me to not follow my instincts and then move in on a vulnerable woman for yourself."

"I told you what was in your best interests. What happened between me and Ariel, it was planned and I'm starting to second guess it. You should second guess yourself. Ariel is wanting to jettison the music career and become a killer."

"No."

"If I don't train her, she's going to be more vulnerable than she's ever been."

"I don't like it."

"And you think I do?"

Matthew hated it when Stone was right. Ariel was going through something none of them understood. He would call in his psychiatrist. He refused to institutionalize Ariel. It was the one thing he knew would destroy her.

She needed help. Sedation was a band aid over a much deeper problem. She was more than a wounded bird. She was an amazing musician. Sharp as a tack and she could be very funny.

He was once a prodigy. He wrote and composed music.

He made a major mistake when he became involved with a woman. Not just any woman, but one married to someone from this world.

Gerald was the only man willing to help save Matthew from his youthful indiscretions. He took Matthew under his wing and groomed him to be his consigliere.

Gerald taught him how to maneuver through the minefield that he had unwittingly stepped into with her. Gerald had been his protector. After the initial threat, the husband of the married woman backed down.

He wanted to be that for Ariel. He had recklessly confessed his emotions. Still waters ran deep after all.

Stone wanted to protect her.

There was a lot posturing going on between the two of them. The fact was Stone had the upper hand. Ariel had given herself to him.

It made his stomach turn just to think about it. Matthew took solace in the fact that it was him and him alone that could reach into her heart of darkness and bring her back to the land of the living when her mind and heart failed her.

"When she's stronger start teaching her. Until then she'll recover under my watchful eye. If she calls out for you, then I'll accept the intrusion. She needs to heal. It's up to me to figure out how to make that happen."

"You're an ass."

"Maybe, but the one thing I know we can agree on is that we love her and want what is best for her."

"If you fuck this up, I don't care how close she is to you. I'll kill you myself," Stone said as he walked away.

"Addy," Ariel murmured.

"She's coming angel. She's coming."

Chapter 9

Beale watched them from a distance. Ever since he had taken his chunk of the business and built on it, Adriana assumed he didn't give a damn about her or Ariel. Nothing could be further from the truth. Once family. Always family.

The truth was he had his ears to the ground and he did not like what he heard where either of them was concerned. Especially Adriana.

Ariel had two fucking morons fighting over her. He loved Stone for the brother he was and if he had to place Ariel with one of the two, it would be him. Matthew was too much of an outsider.

Adriana had been left to fend for herself, and that wasn't fair. She'd lost everything and now to lose her sister too. It was unfathomable.

Ariel had always teetered on the brink. Adriana was with her now. As Adriana comforted her sister he felt a sense of shame wash over him that he hadn't been more present in their lives over the years.

"Addybelle..." Beale said.

Adriana slowly turned. Their eyes met. A longing that he'd never felt before engulfed him. He turned away, disturbed.

Adriana looked down; her own desires stirred up.

"Addy?" Ariel said emerging from the fog. "I love them both. I can't live feeling this way. It's too much pain."

"I'll tell them to back off."

"You will?"

"Of course, I will."

Ariel drifted back to sleep. Adriana approached Beale. "They're killing her."

"I noticed."

"She asked me to tell them to pull back."

"I heard."

"Are we going to talk about it?"

"About what?"

"You're little goombas chasing me around Paris and trying to shake Frankie Galloway's interest in me."

"Talk about a goomba. The guy's slicker than snot."

"He's interested in me. He cares about me. I love Ari, but she seems to captivate everyone else around me. At least with Frankie I'm not wondering if he's going to choose my sister over me."

"I didn't pick your sister over you."

"You just abandoned us both."

Beale's face burned like fire. He knew she was right. It didn't mean he wanted to face it right at the moment.

"I can see that the truth hurts."

"Impossible."

"What are you muttering under your breath?"

"You and your sister are impossible to deal with sometimes."

"What would you know about dealing with me and Ari? You made up your mind a long time ago not to deal with us."

"You're reading the past all wrong."

"Am I?"

"Yes. I take you and your sister's lives into account in everything that I do."

Adriana scoffed. "You chose to say goodbye. When Matthew sent me away you could have fought for me. You could have kept me. I was a good kid, a fast learner. A good judge of character. I would have been an asset to you. But no, you just let Matthew and Stone throw me away like so much trash while they doted on Ari as if she was a lady in waiting."

"Addybelle…"

"Don't Addybelle me. I'm in college. I have my father's brain and my mother's face. I want their respect and sophistication. Instead, when people look at my face all they see is Ariel."

She tried to storm off, he grabbed her hand. "Not me. I see you. I see your ambition. I see the woman you want to be."

"Fuck off," she said wrenching her hand free, getting away this time.

Beale stood there looking after her. He knew the flame that had been lit in him, had been burning in Adriana for a lifetime. He looked back into the room at Ariel. She slept soundly. Well, at least for now.

Pictures of that disastrous night played over and over in his head. Of finding Ariel shot, Matthew near dead, and Adriana raped brutally by someone he'd been hunting for a longtime.

It was a man whose name was avoided at all costs. A man who was not a man but a traitor and a snake. Someone who had coveted Gerald and what he had so much he was obsessed with him and his family.

So much so he had married Kate, Isabel's sister, just to be close to the family. Leo Spencer. One day he would pay for the wrongs he had perpetrated on the twins. And he would be the one to do it.

Chapter 10

Ariel stood, feet apart, hands wrapped around the grip of Stone's gun. Stone stood nearby, keeping an ever-watchful eye on her. She squeezed the trigger. She squeezed again and again.

"That's enough."

Ariel proceeded to unload the weapon in rapid succession.

"I said that's enough."

Her arm dropped to the side, the gun dangling from her hand.

"Hand it to me," Stone held his hand out waiting. "I said hand it to me."

Ariel balked, "Why should I? When I could solve all our problems with just one bullet."

"I see therapy is continuing to do wonders," Stone muttered.

"I haven't had an episode in a month."

"You mean since Matthew triggered you."

"C'mon Stone, you're just mad that there's something he's good at that you're not."

"He confused you."

"It's hard on someone when they're carrying a torch. Cut him some slack."

Stone took the gun and squeezed off five rounds rapidly. "Here, you want to kill yourself? Here's your bullet. I can't do this."

"Can't do what?"

"Listen to you wax prophetic about death. You've cheated it too many times to be cozying up to it again."

"Stone, I know you're hurt-," Ariel said.

"I'm not a fucking little boy. I'm angry. I said I love you because I meant it. I assumed you did too."

"I'm a weird kid. I don't know how to read people. I can't process my emotions properly with people."

"But you can with Matthew."

Ariel turned away.

"That's what I thought. Ariel, either you commit to me, or I go work for Beale."

"You can't."

"I will. It's not in a man like me to fall in love easily. Even less likely to follow you around like a puppy waiting for you to make up your mind."

Ariel slapped him across the face. Tears came to her eyes as she raced away.

Stone loved her, but he knew what she and everyone else did. It was Matthew that made her feel like she was at home and like herself. He was just salt in the wound. Stone had to take care of himself, even if it did rip his heart out to walk away from her.

ARIEL BLEW PAST MATTHEW like a bottle rocket. Matthew had spent his time the last month cooling his heels and trying to let Ariel be Ariel. Knowing she had been there taking lessons from Stone did nothing for his nerves or his heart.

He wasn't one to pontificate on romance. Or love for that matter. But something was rotten. Matthew could smell it. He heard a door slam from the vicinity of the music room or his office. He looked up to see Stone at the end of the hallway.

"I can't do this, only a pussy stands back and waits. I'm sorry she's hurt. A man like me in a world like this only sacrifices when he loves. I don't feel like sacrificing anymore."

"So, you're quitting. On her and on Gerald's legacy."

"Gerald's dead. His legacy is controlled by Beale as we both know. Ariel wants nothing to do with it. Adriana is obsessed with it. Good luck. You were always an afterthought anyway."

Matthew was cold and controlled. "Go to hell, Stone."

Stone vibrated with rage and loss, "You have a beautiful life. When she finally takes her life and believe me, she will. You will have nothing but this big empty house. I, on the other hand, will be fucking my new wife and seducing my girlfriend. Because being a saint has gotten me nothing – absolutely nothing."

Matthew watched him retreat. As soon as he heard the front door close, he roared wordlessly and hurled his coffee cup against the library wall.

From a distance he felt Ariel's heart breaking. Matthew inhaled deeply. He listened closely as he walked towards the music room to put both their hearts back together.

Chapter 11

Ariel stood before the window with a distant look in her eyes. Blank sheet paper all around her. Matthew stood behind her. Willing her to turn around and chase the demons away.

"Angel," he whispered. "I'm sorry."

She said nothing.

She stooped to the ground, staring at all the sheet paper around. "As a kid I just wanted to write and make music. All Addy ever wanted was to be like mom and dad. Sophisticated like mom, powerful and respected like dad."

"You two were inseparable."

"We were. Until that night. The one constant we had was each other. The three of you made choices that took it from us."

"I really don't know what to say."

Ariel looked up and their eyes locked. "The night you and I were shot and left for dead; there was a moment earlier in the evening when I thought, one day, this is what I want it to be like when I fall in love."

Matthew walked towards her. The despair radiated from deep within her, drawing him to her as it always had. He remembered the night in question well. Matthew recalled being charmed by the imp at the piano who was oblivious to the darkness around her. Ariel was a light shining brightly that night. Leo and everyone who had survived had managed to dim that light.

"You set your drink down. And started playing piano with me. It was like you spoke a language that only I could hear. It's always been like that with Addy. But everyone else was always on the outside looking in. It was like you cracked the code and imprinted yourself on my future. I just didn't know it at the time. Then the violence came forever changing me. I have never gotten over it."

Matthew stooped next to her. "I'm sorry I put you in this position,"

"It's not your fault Stone walked away from me. I am. I failed to make a decision in time."

"You deserve to be happy. No matter what that means. Whether it's with Stone or not. Whether it's with me or someone else. You deserve to have what that little girl dreamed of before that horrible night."

Ariel fell to the ground. Matthew eased down next to her. She leaned against him. His arms wound around her.

"I'm blocked. I can't write. The music has stopped singing to me. I love Stone. But he never spoke to me the way your harmony did that night."

"I'm an attorney."

"A musician deep inside."

Ariel and Matthew locked gazes. Ariel could hear the piano keys playing a dark romantic melody. They leaned in close. Matthew heard the harmony. Their lips touched and violins entered the foreground. He deepened the kiss as Ariel curled closer inhaling and tasting his essence. He broke the kiss and they gazed at each other for a long time.

Their mouths clashed, thirsty for each other. A long, heated kiss to absorb the other. Passion unleashed for the first time as they tore each other's clothes from their skin.

Matthew rolled her to her back as he took her breast in his mouth and suckled at it relentlessly, then repeated on her other one.

When he kissed her again, his penis hardened. He longed to bury himself deep inside of her and claim her. He never wanted her to ache or long for another man again.

Ariel warmed to him. He trailed kisses down her body until he buried his face between her legs. As he feasted on her flesh and parried his tongue in and out of her she called out for him uninhibitedly. She bucked and gyrated, climaxing.

"I want to feel you," she gasped. "I need you. I need you inside of me."

He kissed the length of her body and slowly entered her waiting warmth. Together they moved and their passion transcended the physical. The music Ariel had longed to hear came through symphony as they made love, filling the once blank sheets of music with songs to be written about their relationship. A story to be told of their love.

Ariel called out his name and for the first time Matthew gave his heart away to someone who understood him.

As they lay together in the afterglow he said, "You have my heart angel. I will stop at nothing to have yours."

"Who knows how long I've been denying you and me. But I will deny you no longer." Ariel rolled him to his back and straddled him. Slowly she began to rock against him.

Matthew ran his hands up her body and cupped her breasts and he began to worship at her altar.

Soon they came in a frenzied madness of lust, cravings, obsession, and imprinted love. Into the night they worshipped until they collapsed from exhaustion. Knowing they would never feel this way about any other again.

Chapter 12

Chunks of grief, joy, and ecstasy echoed in the darkness completely breaking Matthew's slumber. The music stopped then commenced again. A pen scratched in the interim. Followed by more notes. Ariel sat at the piano completely engrossed in composing.

Her scent surrounded him. Sitting up he pulled on his boxers and slacks and joined her on the piano bench.

"You're writing."

"Your love unlocked my heart. Now everything is just bombarding me. I'm trying to catch it on paper before it disappears."

He kissed her temple.

She paused what she was doing and handed him a pen. "It's been ages, I couldn't possibly keep up with you."

"When we were making love, you heard it too. I know you did. I could see it in the way that you looked at me. Feel it in the way you touched me. Hear it in the way you said my name."

Slowly he took the pen, and as she strung together the melody of their love on the top line, he answered in harmony below. Time seemed to disappear, and they weren't two people collaborating, they were one musical soul, penning an epic musical. Song after song they penned. And for the first time in ages both of them found joy in what they were doing.

The world might reject them in polite society, but one day it would embrace their creation born from a night of passion. Ariel would see her dream come true of performing on Broadway.

"Thank you," she said gazing at him. "This is all I've ever wanted. Except maybe to have my mom and dad and brothers back."

"You have an aunt and a brother."

"Aunt Kate is poison and Zach hasn't come around in ages. Sometimes I think that's been for the best. Sometimes I wish he was still the big brother I remember that doted on both me and Adriana."

"I screwed up so much with you girls."

"I'm not a girl anymore."

Matthew chuckled. "Clearly."

"And you're not the consigliere that my dad groomed you to be."

"I am. But you speak to the part of me that isn't. A part of me that I thought I shut away years ago."

"I've loved you for so long. Since that night everything changed. I know it had to be different for you. I was a child. Addy was a child. You were our guardian."

Matthew thought about it. An image of Ariel on her eighteenth birthday popped into his mind. "I think it started about a year ago. You and Adriana always dressed up on the anniversary of the massacre. I just remember you standing at the top of the staircase. In a vintage white Cinderella strapless ball gown. Black satin gloves to your elbows, your hair swept up off your neck. Your neck adorned with Stone's birthday gift of an Algerian replica love knot necklace from Casino Royale. My breath caught. I felt my feelings of friendship start to shift. That's when I think, at least subconsciously, things started to change for me."

"It's always been you and Stone. For different reasons. But now, it's only you."

"No shift?"

"For me, the realization that I had to choose one of you was awful. I realized I couldn't be selfish. I didn't even really decide. Stone chose for us by walking away. It was then I knew if I loved him the way he loved me, I would take every opportunity to run towards him. Instead, I ran towards the music and that's where you waited for me."

Matthew took her hand and kissed it.

"My loyalty is first and foremost always to you."

"You swear?"

"As long as you feel the same way neither of us will feel romantic pain again."

"No pain," Ariel whispered.

"No pain," Matthew whispered back.

They kissed tenderly. Then turned to the piano and began to sing and play, lost in their own little world. Protected from the ugly reality that danger was ever present. Stone's departure could bring the pain the five of them had been trying to avoid since Christmas Eve thirteen years ago.

Chapter 13

Matthew sat in his office taking his afternoon tea while listening to Ariel perfect the musical they had birthed a week ago. A smile touched his lips. His phone rang. He sighed and picked up the receiver.

"Matthew Gershwin."

"You sonofabitch!" Matthew knew that ball of anger.

"You're a fine one to talk, Scott."

"She was mine."

"Scott, you should know, no one owns Ariel, least of all a weak, spineless man like you."

"You and that gorilla pass her back and forth like a damn football."

"You'd do well to speak of a woman you claim to love with a great deal more respect."

"We were the glory of the music circuit."

"Things change Scott."

"They don't."

"Ariel was dying you fucking arrogant prick. You drove her into Stone's arms. All she wants is stability and to be loved and you can't give that to her."

"And you can?"

"I'm a man. You're a boy."

"For all you're posturing, you can't keep her safe. You mistake me for a normal, weak boy, but I can reach where even you can't. She rejected me. I will find a way to destroy her."

Matthew's spine straightened. A darkness that existed within him emerged. "If you hurt her, if she sheds one tear, you'd better pray her family never hears of it. And when I say family, I mean me. Are we crystal?"

"Big talk. We'll see when the moment comes what you're actually capable of."

Then, there was a dial tone.

Shit.

He didn't want to invite Stone in, or Beale. But the fact was Scott had just declared war on all of them.

If Scott lived in their world he wouldn't hesitate to take the punk out himself. Scott wasn't a threat in and of himself. But his mother was always looking to get a toe in the criminal world. She was calculating and ambitious.

She was what Beale called a slummer. She was a bored ambassador's wife. She was the problem. Her family connections reached into their circles. A distant cousin of Leo's she was a potential bomb waiting for her pin to be pulled.

The music had stopped.

He rubbed his eyes and looked up and the love of his life stood there. "Want to grab a picnic lunch and head out onto the terrace?"

He couldn't help but smile. "Get Sophie to put some cheese and wine together and I'll meet you there."

Ariel walked into the office. She started humming. She sang her question to him.

"What's wrong my love?"

"Nothing for you to worry about."

"I need to know what's going on."

"Scott threatened the family."

"He threatened me, didn't he?"

"Yes. I have to increase security."

"Stone's not going to come back. I've burned that bridge."

"Stone has always been loyal to the Stuarts. Nothing is going to change that."

"He's a man. He has his pride."

"He will come back to protect you. He won't deny you."

"Is that fair?"

"I don't give a damn about fair. I give a damn about you."

Ariel touched his face. "You gave me my life back. I swear my allegiance to you and my sister. To Beale and Stone. But my heart belongs to you."

"And mine to you. Now go get that picnic ready for us."

Ariel straddled him in his chair. They kissed as she moved against his body. He pressed his face against her neck and moved her ass in rhythm to her grind, and for the moment he let go and they climaxed, his name falling from her lips, as his love for her fell from his.

Chapter 14

The phone rang.

The woman next to Beale groaned. "Who is that at this time in the morning?"

Beale rubbed his eyes and looked at the clock. It read 3AM. He grabbed the receiver. "Matthew this had better be an emergency."

"Since you have cut me off otherwise; I had no other choice."

"Matthew this is the first time in ages that I could close my eyes."

"There's a new threat to the girls. The responsibility of it lies at my feet. But it requires an expertise only you can address."

"I always knew you were too soft for this world."

"I am interested in giving Ariel a normal life. She will never have that if Scott is sniffing around and-"

"I am not making Stone watch you love his heartbreak."

"Scott called and point blank threatened her."

"That pipsqueak I'm sure you can handle him."

"You not hearing me. It's not the pipsqueak I'm worried about. It's his relative."

Beale lay prone for a moment. Then turned to the woman. "You need to go."

She shifted.

"Stone will take you home. Let me get to my office."

Beale slipped in his clothes and headed to his den.

MATTHEW LISTENED CLOSELY; Ariel was working. The strains of what they had created only days ago. He stood up and let the notes pull him in. Then her voice, that beautiful angelic voice cracked his heart open as she sang out her heartbreak over all that she had lost in her life.

He sauntered into the room and began singing the harmony to her melody. He took her hand and led her to her feet. He started the metronome and they began to waltz.

Ariel grinned and asked, "What are you worried about?"

"What do you mean?"

"As a kid, whenever you were scared for our safety, you would waltz with me to calm me down."

"Hmm. Dancing with you as a little girl versus now is very different."

"I understand that. But it doesn't change the fact that you're scared. I can see the fear in your eyes."

"My darling angel, how can you tell that?"

"I know you like you know me."

Matthew smiled as they waltzed through the room the metronome ticking to each step. "It surprises me how much sometimes."

"I knew Stone. And all I did was hurt him. I hurt you too."

"We're passed that."

"Promise."

"Well, I am worried."

"It's Scott."

"Get out of here."

"He says he's going to bring you pain. That he's going to bring me pain. I fear I can't protect you."

"You're hesitating. What aren't you telling me?"

"I've reached out to Beale and Stone for help."

Ariel slowed to a stop.

"No."

"Ariel, please."

"You've got to prove to Beale you aren't dependent on him. Otherwise, he'll see you as weak and unable to protect anyone."

"Listen, I could give a shit what Beale thinks of me. I just care about keeping you safe."

"And I love you to pieces for it. Is it fair to ask Stone to enter this world again?"

"This world isn't about fair. It's about survival. If you can scratch a piece of land and love for yourself you hold on as tight as you can. Fair is what you make of it."

"It's hard not to feel guilty."

"Try not to. Stone is out drowning his sorrows in drink and women."

"He's not happy."

"Are you not happy?"

"I am ecstatic with you. But a part of me is always a little sad."

"This musical is going to change your life."

"It might not happen if people see Stone skulking around you."

"We'll keep you safe, we'll make it happen. And you won't have to be sad and guilty anymore."

As the metronome ticked back and forth they resumed their private waltz. Ariel began to sing. Matthew became enraptured all over again.

Chapter 15

"A party?" Adriana asked.

Ariel turned around and faced her sister. "Yes, an investors party. We'll be performing some of the more polished pieces from the musical."

"And the musical is about our family?"

"In part. It's about me and what made me fall in love with Matthew."

"You're out of your mind."

"Beale has already agreed to it."

"That's because he never could say no to your whims. Me on the other hand he's more than happy to say no to me."

"I wish I could change that for you. So, tell me about this guy Frankie. Is he Beale's replacement?"

"No one could replace Beale."

"This guy makes you happy though, right?"

"Yes, but you should know better than anybody there's happy and then there's happy."

"I loved Stone. I knew Stone. But not in the way I did Matthew."

"As far as I'm concerned neither of them deserve you. However, Stone can protect you. Matthew answers something in you the way that something in Beale calls to me. Maybe it's wrong. Maybe it's bad. Maybe it's selfish. Maybe it's wrong. But neither of us can help it."

"No, we can't."

"So, to answer your question, Frankie Galloway is a friend. And he only cares about me and isn't worried about his empire or, no offense, you."

"And to answer yours, yes, a party. A masquerade party."

"Then let's prepare to drive them wild while emptying their pockets."

"Definitely."

Both women laugh conspiratorially and start to get ready.

MATTHEW LOOKED HIMSELF over in the mirror. A Gucci tuxedo and phantom mask with a rose across the nose and cheek that Ariel had chosen. He fingered the mask and smiled.

"You've never looked so self-satisfied."

Matthew didn't look up. Stone was there. As broody and angry as ever. "You're not doing this for me."

"No, I'm not. Ariel has dreamed of going to Broadway for a long time. I could never do that for her. I couldn't unblock her. Though I'm loathe to say it. You understood that. You know how to do the second thing. Tonight is a testament of that song inside of her that has charmed us both for a while now."

"I'm not one for confrontation, but do not exploit Ariel's guilt."

"I'm not a little boy. I care about Ariel. I love her. I won't hurt her. But make no mistake the minute you hurt her, I'll make good on my promise to pick up the pieces."

"Is that a threat?"

"It is what it is. Men like you are weak. You can't handle a woman like Ariel. Because this world will eventually eat you alive."

Matthew grew cold. "Stay in your lane Ramsey or you will see how dangerous I really am."

"Is everything okay in here?" Adriana asked.

Matthew smiled, "Yes, it is."

Adriana looked to Stone, who said nothing.

"Play nice, my sister's heart is on the line. I won't have either of you shattering it."

Ariel appeared. "Matthew?"

"My god, you look like an angel."

He took her in his arms.

"He's right," Stone said. Adriana gave him a pitiful look. He turned and left the office.

"You two should be more considerate. Especially you, Matthew."

"He should get a pair of balls and use them," Mathew said.

"It would serve you right if Ariel broke your heart."

"Addy!"

Adriana sighed. She grabbed her sister's hand and squeezed. "You are beautiful. Go knock them dead."

Adriana left the room and Matthew swept Ariel's body against his. "I love you. I don't care who knows it."

"I love you too."

Matthew kissed her and led her out to the party. He prayed Stone's presence didn't backfire on him. Ariel had a soft heart. He was now point. Stone was going to fight for her in his way. Two warriors. One queen.

Chapter 16

Ariel was more alive than she'd ever been. She practically glowed as she and Matthew waltzed to the sounds of her demo songs playing in the background. The ballroom buzzed about Ariel. Everyone but Stone who drank shots at a table as he watched the couple.

"She's shining isn't she," Beale said. "I don't think I've ever seen her so happy."

"Go to hell."

Stone tried to stand.

"You could have said no to the assignment."

Stone's anger leveled him. "You know better than that."

Beale's gaze drifted over to Adriana who was busy charming Senator Lake and his wife Tasha. "I guess I do. Gerald tied our fates together long ago."

"The night Leo ambushed the family we got a lot dumped in our laps."

Beale looked pained, he turned to Stone and said, "I remember Adriana that night. I know what that bastard did to her. She thinks I don't know or care. It has to be that way. I don't care that she hates me. As long as Leo never touches her again, as long as she's safe..."

Stone did another shot of bourbon.

"I don't feel as generous. I want Ariel for myself. I know a part of her loves me. That part that is cold, dark and afraid of being hurt. I'm a pain killer. Matthew is her music maker, they can collaborate."

"And you hate him for it," Beale said chuckling, "Have another shot, but don't get too sloppy. We still need you to keep us safe."

"Let me tell you, I'm fucking thrilled about that."

Suddenly all the air left the room and conversations halted.

Everyone turned their heads as Adriana walked in on Frankie Galloway's arm. Beale's countenance darkened. He set his drink down.

"Don't be stupid Beale."

"You sit and drink. I'm going to keep Adriana from doing something stupid."

Stone kept throwing back shots. His high tolerance for alcohol didn't bode well for anyone in his circle when the time came for them to be punished.

Even though his anger remained, he didn't wish to punish Ariel. He wanted to keep her close. To keep her safe and sound. As long as Matthew lived and breathed he couldn't. Not in the way he wanted. Stone would be damned if he let anyone see him bleed over it.

FRANKIE WHISPERED IN Adriana's ear. "Don't look now, but the big bad wolf approaches."

"I guess he's going to try to mark his territory."

"Adriana, you look well," Beale said.

"Like you give a damn."

"Addybelle, do we have to do this here. You came to your sister's party on this common thug's arm. Isn't that a bit of a slap in the face?"

"To whom? Ariel? Hardly. You? Definitely. As for being a common thug, the only thing that elevates you is my father's money which you used to build what is rightfully mine. As for Addybelle, she died that night more than thirteen years ago. Frankie, let's find Ari. I want to have some fun."

Frankie shook his head and smiled as they walked away. Beale looked back at Stone. He raised his glass. Beale looked toward the entrance. There stood the most unwanted couple. Harbingers of ill will and nothing of good to come of their presence, Zachary Spencer and his mother Kate entered and smiled.

Beale looked back to Stone. Stone nodded. This was Ariel's night. He hated Matthew with every fiber of his being; he would not let these two destroy her happiness ever again.

Chapter 17

Matthew stared at who had just walked into the room. Ariel was at the piano readying the music. He had a flashback to that night he had tickled the ivories with a child. A child who had grown into very different woman.

In part because of the woman and man who called themselves family on the other side of the room. His eyes met Stone's.

"What is it?" she asked him.

He flashed a charming and tender smile. "Nothing my darling. Let us dazzle the crowd we have assembled."

Ariel felt the hairs standing on the back of her neck. Her instincts told her something was about to happen. Something very wrong and something very bad. Something like thirteen years ago.

She ignored her gut and started playing. Matthew came in with the harmony and together they sang the triumphant love song, "When I Saw You."

You could have heard a pin drop. The audience was transfixed. Ariel gazed at Matthew. She knew she would love him forever and that he felt the same way about her.

They played and played, weaving a magical spell over themselves and the audience. A loud bang pierced the magic and Matthew fell forward. His blood sprayed across the sheet music. Women screamed.

Ariel trembled. Hers and Matthew's love cut short. She sang the most painful part of the musical in a desperate attempt to keep him alive. He wouldn't die if she just kept singing.

She cradled him in her arms. He looked at her as the light faded from his eyes. He touched her face ever so lightly. Her singing became choked and broken.

His hand fell away. Her cheek smeared with his blood. Her dress ruined with it. Suddenly his eyes slid shut. Stone jerked her up and out of the room.

Beale turned to Frankie, "Get her out of here."

Adriana led Frankie in Stone and Ariel's direction into the study and locked the door.

"I don't mean to criticize your security detail, but it seems Leo's decoys did their job."

"Oh, shut the fuck up Galloway."

Ariel had a thousand-yard stare. She didn't cry. She didn't move. It seemed like any soul she had ever had finally left her body. She looked at Adriana.

"Addy. Addy. Addy."

"I understand a direct hit on the girls. But Matthew, a lawyer? That's unusual," Frankie said. "I mean I'd expect Stone to die before Matthew."

"Stone wasn't the intended target. Scott wanted to make Ari hurt. He wanted to destroy her. So, he took from her what he wanted to be."

"Damn it."

"Scott is as duplicitous as his uncle is."

"Come on Adriana, help me get the two of you into the main panic room and get her cleaned up."

ARIEL SAT IN THE TUB. She stared down into the water and saw his reflection.

Their joyous night together. All their plans and their lives were laid out before them. The magic of their lovemaking. The brutality of it being snatched away.

The tears that she didn't shed in the moment, now came easily and dissipated her great love's image. She began sobbing. Then she wailed. Her heart had been ripped out and it was still beating. She began keening. It felt as if she would die from it and that she had no reason to continue.

First, her parents and her brothers. Now her lover. Her best friend, confidant and collaborator.

She looked up and there stood Stone with a robe. She had no right to ask anything of him. He stood there as always, offering his quiet brand of comfort.

She looked to him expectantly shivering from the cold and the grief. He went to her and stood her up. Stone wrapped her in the towel and lifted her out of the tub. Ariel laid her head onto his shoulder and said, "I'm going to kill Scott, and you're going to show me how to do it."

Chapter 18

Ariel led the funeral profession. She walked along the horse drawn casket, her hand on the coffin.

Hundreds of onlookers lined the streets, crying as if they knew him as she did. They did not.

Near her stood Adriana. She walked hand in hand with her. Adriana had always hated Matthew, thought him weak. But the bottom line was she only wanted Ariel to be happy. And with Matthew, Ariel had been happy.

They had already endured unimaginable losses. Ari had never quite recovered from them. Ariel was a force at times, showing flashes of what she could be on stage. It had been seven days since Matthew died. Ariel had drunk little and eaten less. If someone had asked she would have told them she was dead inside.

Adriana worried that Ariel, who had always walked the razor's edge of sanity, had lost her anchor.

Ariel walked in a black vintage Valentino mourning type gown accompanied with a long, sheer black veil.

Adriana wore the same-except in white. She clasped her sister's hand and looked back at the two men following them. She thought if she ever lost Beale she would rage and spin out of control like a lunatic. Though she didn't care for Stone, she knew he was Ari's only hope.

Beale and Stone kept a respectful distance.

"She hasn't come out of her room for seven days," Beale said.

"I know," Stone said.

"Are you glad she's free of him?"

"No, it's turning her into something I always feared she might become."

"And what's that?"

"A blind killer."

"You think she's got that in her?"

"I know she does, she's given me the order to turn her into one in Matthew's name."

"That doesn't mean you have too."

Stone looked at Beale and said, "Yes it does."

Stone then proceeded to close in on Ariel. From then on she would be his only concern. He would protect the family. She would mourn Matthew. He himself rued the day Gerald ever brought him into the circle of confidentiality.

Everyone had left the church leaving Ariel with Matthew's casket. She knew when she left the building she would not be looking back. She would be saying goodbye forever.

In the back of the church, she knew she had an audience. She knew it was one person. It was Stone.

"It's okay."

Ariel jumped and looked up. It was Matthew. Or his ephemeral apparition. He reached out his hand.

"Ariel, my beloved. I will always be here."

"Not with me."

"I will always be watching over you."

"You promised me forever."

"Someone took it from us."

"You know who took it from us."

"Scott."

"A wannabe Machiavelli."

"He's not that subtle," Ariel said.

"Maybe not, but I need for you to be smart in your vengeance. I know Stone doesn't care for me, but I know he loves you. Don't be afraid to ask for his help."

"We were supposed to be happy and live that way forever."

He touched her cheek and kissed her temple. "I know it's all far, far from fair. But don't be foolish and get yourself killed. You can get the revenge you want and still have the soft place to fall you need."

He gazed into her eyes then stood as if to go.

She reached for him. Matthew faded away like the ghost he was. It felt as if a sharp knife plunged into her heart. The pain ripped through her heart and soul and cut her in two. She cried out in agony and Stone came up to her and wrapped her in his coat and swept her up in his arms.

As the candles burned.

And Ariel stared at the altar murmuring, "Goodbye, Matthew. I'll make this right. I promise."

Chapter 19

Ariel was locked in her room. She had refused to come out. Beale had tried to coax her out, as had Adriana. Stone now stood dutifully outside her door. She knew Adriana was probably dealing with memories of their family's demise. Beale would help her. She knew Stone was on the other side of the door. He respected her need to grieve and kept his distance.

Ariel looked at her bedside table. Bottles of bipolar medication were in a line neatly next to her prized photo of Matthew and her performing together.

She didn't want to continue. She thought about having hit the sweet spot with hers and Matthew's creation.

It was one month. Their romantic relationship had lasted one month and felt like days.

They had spent hours at a time making love. Hours at a time in the shower. Hours creating together.

Now she had one purpose. It was no longer to put on a performance or happily tour the world. It was to find that pea-brained, skinflint, duplicitous spawn from Leo's family tree - Scott.

Find him and shoot him between the eyes. Leave him for dead. Leave those around him broken-hearted.

She wasn't just broken-hearted. She was dead inside. She had been for so long. Matthew had always brought her such joy. She stared at her line of bipolar meds.

Matthew always made it a part of her routine to take her meds. Now she no longer cared. What little light there had been in her life was gone. She wanted to die. That was all she wanted to do was die.

A wave of nausea overtook her. She raced to the balcony and retched violently. Vomit erupted from her so fast, and so hard that she was unable to balance herself properly.

Ariel tried to hold on, but she could feel herself threatening to go overboard. The door opened and a hand pulled her back from the ledge and set her down on her feet. She turned around. There was Stone. Stone had always been there.

"I'm sorry."

"Now's not the time for that."

"Can we go practice?"

"You're too emotional tonight. You just lost Matthew. Matthew wouldn't understand you killing for him. But I do. When your moment comes to take Scott out, I want you to be prepared. I don't want him to win the war. He may have won this round but that's temporary."

"How do you do it?"

"Do what?"

"Stay strong in the face of it all."

"I don't let myself feel."

"But you feel with me."

"Against my better judgement."

"There's something I was going to tell Matthew. I was so excited. We were going to keep it to ourselves. Now I have to tell you. Because without your help I'm afraid...I'm afraid, what little hope or light in my life will vanish."

"What are you talking about?"

Ariel walked past Stone and into her bathroom. There was a pregnancy test on the sink. She stared at it for the longest time before Stone showed up behind her. She looked at his reflection.

He saw the test. "You're pregnant."

"Yes."

"Am I the father or is Matthew?"

"Truth. I can't be sure."

"You want it to be his though."

"I'm sure a piece of me does. Just as I'm sure a piece of me wants it to be yours."

"You don't have to lie to me."

"I want it to be Matthew's. I need it to be his. I know I'm selfish for wanting it to be that way."

"Tell me what to do Ariel."

"Be my partner. Keep this child safe. Raise him in your image. With my heart. With Matthew's savvy. Let him or her be the best of all of us."

"Command me."

"I command you."

"Then it is so."

Chapter 20

"What do you mean she's pregnant?!" Beale exclaimed.

"They were in love. They were adults. What did you expect her to do with him? Play tiddlywinks?" Adriana spat out.

"I was under the impression that she was in love with Stone."

Stone stood quietly by the door.

"She was," Adriana said pointedly.

"Then why did she love Matthew?"

"They both answered something unique to them inside of her."

"Your sister was selfish."

Adriana stood defiantly, "My sister was torn. In a way she still is. She had only one thing of Matthew's - their child. It's the only thing keeping her tethered to this earth. It makes me scream when idiots like you don't understand."

"I just bet it does."

"Your sarcasm is wasted on me, Beale. You could have had me and you wasted that opportunity. Don't shit on my sister in the process. Or I will cut you so deep you won't know what hit you."

Stone leans forward. "Who she loves or loved makes no difference. We now have another generation of Stuarts to protect."

"That's rather cold," Beale said.

"That's the practical reality of the situation."

"He's not wrong Beale. But he's still a cold bastard."

Adriana walked out of the den and took a few deep breaths, then headed to her sister's room.

She walked into Ariel's room. "Ari?" Adriana didn't see her.

Scanning the room, she noticed the door partially open to the balcony. She walked over to check it. Ariel sat curled up in her chair beneath a pile of Matthew's coats, her face buried in them.

"Oh Ariel," she said stepping forward.

"Don't come any closer."

"He's not here Ari."

"You think I don't know that?" Ariel snapped.

"I leave in a few days. I have a life in Paris waiting for me. I know Matthew was the **One** for you. But he's gone. You can't hide like this forever. I won't be here to shield you from Beale and Stone."

"I don't need shielding from them. I need them to turn me into a killer."

"Ariel, don't say that."

"The only thing that matters is this baby Matthew left me. I don't even know if I'm going to be a good mother. If I deserve to have any piece of Matthew."

"You did, you do."

"How can you be so sure?"

"Even though I think he was a schmuck, he was the only one who ever shattered the darkness around you. He knew how to make you happy. It's why Stone couldn't oust him out of your heart. Now Matthew left you his son or daughter to bring the light. I know the next nine months are going to bring you a total eclipse of the heart. You're going to swallow that blackness and banish it to the depths of hell once that child is born. But until then, you're going to embrace it and your love for Stone."

Breathing Matthew's scent Ariel thought to the night they conceived this new life. She could feel the sheet music. Her skin on his. The ecstasy and fire he brought out in her.

The tenderness and anticipation she felt as he moved inside her. The way they had become one. The way he had breathed her name and promised her forever.

She choked on her sobs for a minute, and let herself be consumed by her grief for a while longer. Finally, she dried her eyes and swallowed her pain, locking it in an invisible safe with a heart carved with Matthew's and her initials.

Stone appeared. Ariel removed the coats and stood.

"I'm ready."

"Indeed you are," Stone said and held out his arm.

She took it, and together they made their way to the gun range and began the business of turning her into a killer.

Chapter 21

They took their dinner in silence.

Ariel ate Sofia's delectable chicken dinner as if it were her last meal.

They had been shooting all morning. There wasn't much to say. It wasn't like she'd forgotten the man she loved. It was more than that, if she allowed herself to think about Matthew she would sink into dark despair. That was a luxury she could not afford with the baby coming at the end of the year.

As much as she wanted to drown her sorrows in mimosas, there was the baby's health to continue.

Stone was before her. She caressed her stomach; she had an appointment for an amniocentesis today.

On a visceral level she knew this child was Matthew's. The more time she spent with Stone at the gun range, the more she was forced to remember their night of passion shortly before embracing her true love for Matthew.

Oh, had their night of passion been something to remember! She had easily locked it away while Matthew was alive, but the more she embraced the darkness of *the Life*. The more she remembered her love for Stone. The more she wished she weren't pregnant and trying to determine paternity of this child.

She wanted easy and simple. Not hard and complicated. She had always loved Matthew, then fell in love with him.

Ariel hero worshipped Stone as a child. Then was annoyed by him. Then loved him. He wasn't a therapist dragging her into the light. He was the part of her who understood vengeance, and was willing to help her get it.

Matthew had been her light and her chance at leaving this world behind. Now she was chained to it. She would be until the day she died.

"Are you okay?" Stone asked her.

"Just scared."

"Of what exactly?"

She held his gaze. Ariel could always be sure of one thing with Stone. They would always tell each other the truth. So, even if she wasn't interested in love or passion with him, their relationship as friends always stood true.

"I'm afraid of what the amnio is going to say."

"That it's mine."

"I know you don't want to hear this, but I don't want it to be. A part of me is hoping he or she will be the redemption I need after I kill the man who took their father from me."

"Don't worry. I've never thought I'd have a legacy to speak of, never thought I'd live this long. Let alone have a child. I dedicated my life to your family a long time. You and your child"s safety are my only concern at this point."

"Funny, if I weren't pregnant, I'd just give in to all this pain."

"Is it wise to think like that?"

"I can only numb myself for so long."

Stone took her hand.

"I am here for you. You know how I feel about you. I've committed my whole life specifically to you. I understand that Matthew offered you something I can't. But if you'll have me, I'm yours."

He touched her baby bump.

"Even killers can love," he said. "You'll have vengeance. I can give you you're happily ever after. It will just be a little darker. I promise, this child will know how much their father loved them."

Tears fell down Ariel's cheeks.

She stood and said with a trembling voice, "Come with me."

And together they walked to her room and shut the door. She gazed into his eyes and said, "Make me forget the pain. Just for a little while."

Stone lifted her legs and pinned her against the door. And together they pretended it was true love, even though it wasn't.

Chapter 22

Ariel reached for Stone, but he was already gone. Her eyes closed. There was something different about her this morning. She sat up and called for him.

"Stone?"

She scanned the room. He was gone. She sighed. The night before was something of a blur. She had wanted to forget for a little while and Stone had obliged her.

She'd selfishly taken him up on his feelings for her. She tried to feel guilty but the truth was she felt nothing. She was numb. That was a relief.

The pain over the loss of Matthew had been so great she couldn't function. Sleeping with Stone was a little band aid over a much bigger wound. For now, it would have to do. Losing Matthew had broken her beyond repair.

Having Stone would keep her alive. Stone would allow her to have her revenge. He would allow her to become the killer she needed to be in order to make peace with the demons in her heart, mind, and soul.

She listened closely, the sound of a shower running greeted her ears.

The lovemaking had knocked her out and allowed Ariel a peaceful night's sleep for once since Matthew's death. Sleep had been nothing but memories of a better time. Her brief time with her husband had taught her you take nothing for granted.

She may have been numb, but she knew she loved Stone. Not in the way she had been besotted with Matthew, but she had been in love with him just the same. Just as Matthew and she had been musical soulmates, Ariel realized Stone and she were connected in bloodshed.

She climbed out of bed and stripped out of her nightgown. Naked she walked to the bathroom connected to her room and walked through the door, stepping behind Stone and pressing her body to his, she touched his stomach and they quivered and groaned.

"Ariel..."

She took his cock in her hand and lovingly stroked it. He hardened and whirled around slamming her to the wall, thrusting inside her to his hilt. His gaze bored into her. His passions laid bare and his love obvious to her.

She loved him too. But she couldn't quite say it. Couldn't quite bring herself to feel it. But this, being with him, smelling his skin. Feeling him inside of her, pumping in and out of her savagely trying to claim her was erotic. She could bring herself to let go enough and enjoy.

The results of the amniocentesis would be in later in the day.

She would ponder over Matthew and hers coming bundle of joy then. Right now, she let Stone show her that lovemaking and savage fucking could be one and the same.

Orgasm after orgasm overwhelmed her until she was shouting Stone's name and inevitably the truth come to the surface and tears rolled down her cheeks.

As she came she chanted like a sea ravaged mermaid, "I love you Stone. I love you. I need blood. I need Scott's blood. I still love Matthew. But I love you now. I honor you now."

"As I honor you, my love."

He swallowed her with his kiss and ravaged her body with his touch. Ariel remembered and forgot at the same time and she came until she quivered. They were breathless.

Their lips inches apart. "Let's go kill someone," he said.

Ariel came again.

"Let's go kill Scott."

"Your wish. My command."

They kissed, and in that moment they were bonded forever.

"I love you Stone."
"And I love you, I have always loved you."

Chapter 23

"I really don't like this," Beale said.

"It's not a matter of what you like," Stone said. "It's a matter of what will keep her alive."

"I know what's keeping her alive, I heard you two all night long."

Stone went rigid. "Watch. Your. Mouth."

"You're fucking the legacy. How is that supposed to work? She just lost Matthew. As much as I didn't like him, she's carrying his child. It has now become our focus."

"You are such a fucking hypocrite. You are fixated on Adriana. You know I can keep us all safe."

"Can you? With your mind on fucking her? I seriously doubt you can manage it. Loving her has already cost her Matthew. What do you think she'll do if she loses you too?"

"She won't lose me. The issue at hand is giving her a reason to hang on and not hang herself. Her emotional stability has always been in question."

"The way Adriana and Ariel lost their innocence has made them both reckless. It's made them not give a damn about living or dying."

"Well, at least you're right about one thing. Ariel has always lived with a death wish. Adriana on the other hand wants the whole enchilada. You, her sister's safety, and the business at her fingertips."

"You think that's why she's carrying on with Galloway?"

"No, I think she's doing that to fuck with you."

"Why in the hell would she do that?"

"She loves you. You won't have anything to do with her. She's wants your attention."

"And I should just give into her."

"I don't even know if I'm doing the right thing with Ariel. By the way she has an amniocentesis scheduled today."

"Do you think the baby is yours?" Beale asked.

"I don't know what to think."

"What are you going to do if it's yours?"

"Be the best father I can be."

"And if it's not?"

"I'm not sure how I'll feel about it, but I love that woman. All I want to do is make her happy. If that means raising Matthew's child as my own, I will."

"You're a better man than I," Beale replied.

"I'm keenly aware of that," Stone said laughing.

Beale pulled out a cigar and handed it to Stone, then retrieved one for himself. "For when you get back from the appointment. We'll either celebrate, or I'll console you with a Cuban."

"Rolled on the thighs of a thousand virgins?"

Beale smirked, "Is there any other way?"

Both men laughed. Stone walked away knowing his future would always be entwined with the Stuart twins and Beale Alastair. And now he would be tied to Ariel's child, because, blood or no blood, he had been a part of Ariel's life since forever.

Now he would spend forever loving her and her child.

As he knocked on her door he thought of their moments together. Their passion was almost animal-like. He also loved the quiet moments in-between.

Maybe it wasn't love for Ariel yet. When the child came he intended on proving he was enough. That while it was tragic that Matthew had died he was never made for this world. Ariel deserved more than a life of vengeance.

"Ariel...," he said pushing the door open.

She was sitting on the edge of the bed. Something was wrong.

"What is it?"

"I'm spotting."

Stone walked with a purpose towards her and lifted her up.

"I can't lose this baby."

"You won't," he promised.

And together they rushed into the early morning towards a future, an uncertain one.

But the future, nonetheless.

Chapter 24

Ariel lay curled up sleeping in the hospital bed.

Stone stood over her protectively.

The news wasn't good. She'd lost the baby. Stone worried. He wasn't the sensitive type that Matthew was, but the idea of Ariel would wake to that new reality concerned him. Ariel was barely hanging on as it was.

She looked so small. He'd kept his distance as she'd cried herself to sleep.

Damn, he was so angry. It was impossible to articulate how angry he was. He wasn't someone in touch with his feelings.

Matthew used to call him a savage. The one feeling he seemed to access often and easily was rage. Any tenderness he felt was reserved for Ariel. Grief-laced rage was dangerous.

Not for Matthew, but there had been a chance that child would have been his. Now Ariel would grieve the baby as Matthew's. His own grief would have been denied.

But he was happy to deny his grief for a maybe child. For a future filled with a well-adjusted Ariel. He didn't know if she would love him in the way she loved Matthew. There was an opportunity to be had if he was the one to give her closure. Whatever that opportunity was, he would take it.

Her eyes fluttered open. "Stone?"

He didn't move.

"Something's not right."

He had to remind her of the miscarriage. Rage-filled grief bubbled up inside of him. So, surprisingly did the tears. He took measured steps forward and sat on the bed. He took her hand.

"I'm sorry."
She was pale, sad, and numb. She had cried until she couldn't cry anymore.

She was done with the tears. Done with acknowledging vulnerability and weakness. She knew she could never be whole again. Not with Matthew gone.

She would be a broken vessel with revenge piecing her back together again. Stone would help her. That was the piece of her that Stone knew best. That was her song that sang to him.

The delicate girl had vanished. What there had been left of her died when Matthew died. Stone would be her shield now. Once she became proficient at handling a gun she would be his.

But there was one thing to determine. She and Matthew controlled a chunk of her father's holdings. Part of it was Adriana's. Her mind raced as she wrapped her body around Stone's waist.

"Who do we work for?"

"I've always protected you and worked for Beale. I don't see why that should change."

"It's not me the two of you will contend with."

Stone knew Ariel was right. He also knew Ariel would be loyal to her sister when it came to Beale.

"We'll worry about work and loyalty when you've healed."

"I'm never going to heal."

"Don't say that."

"You realize to heal; I would have to fall in love again. I don't want to ever love someone the way I loved Matthew and our child. Losing them is too much."

Stone turned away.

She touched his face. "I love you in a different way. Loving Matthew came in a much different way. And being that uninhibited about it cost me. It cost me the way it did Dad and Mom. I don't want to lose anyone else, especially you. Beale and Addy will make their way to one another – eventually. Love in our world is dangerous and a luxury. I love you. But I'm going to kill the man who cost me my normalcy. I will bleed from grief forever. From this moment on I will never feel normal or expect to be normal again."

Chapter 25

Ariel woke up in Stone's arms. It was a new day and a new life. She rolled out of bed and stared down at her wedding ring. Stone placed his hand on her back.

"You okay?"

"I'm fine."

She touched the simple gold band, and stood up. "Ariel, you ready for this?"

"More than ever."

She walked up to the mirror. She would have been nine months along by now.

She pushed it out of her mind and slipped into her black jeans and black shirt. Then shoved her feet into her combat boots.

"Stone, I'm a little sore, could you tie them?"
"Yeah, sure."
They moved in the quiet of the room.
"You sure you want to take this step Ariel? Once you take a life you can't go back. It marks you. Maims you. Your soul never quit recovers."
"I've had things stolen from me that I can't get back. What's one more piece of that soul?"

"Right now, you've had everything taken from you. Now you'll be giving your soul away. It doesn't seem very different, but it is."

She holstered her gun and turned to Stone.

"One day I will kill the people responsible for the death of my family. Now we start with the one who took what was left of my heart and destroyed my chance at piecing my soul back together."

"I'm sorry Ariel."

"It's okay Stone. Most people get either redemption or vengeance. This is the hand I've been dealt. It is what it is."

"I just want you to be aware of what's waiting for you out there once you do this. You will be on their radar more so than ever before today."

"You're kidding me right?"

"No. I'm serious."

"I've been a target since the day I was born. Maybe not in the way you are. My name makes me a target. You've been a part of my life since I could walk and chew gum because of that. I used to struggle with that pain of death. I still do. But now I can do something about it."

"Oh."

"Listen, Stone, people underestimate you. They just think you're a blunt instrument. I know better. You're sharp as a tack. Still waters run deep. I love you, Stone. Different from the way I love Matthew. But I love you just as powerfully in that you have a song that calls to me. Matthew's was one of life and living. Yours is of recklessness, danger, and the razor's edge of a death wish. You want to save and protect me. But I don't think anybody can."

"So, I should just let you die?"

"Now, that wouldn't be either of us. As much as I would try to let go, you'll fight to hang on. I wouldn't expect anything else."

"So, you're going to torture me along the way."

Ariel smiled wryly, "I wouldn't say that. But I'm not going to make your job easy. Maybe, who knows, if I can get closure we can do what Matthew and I were going to do."

"What's that?"

"Walk away from the business altogether."

Stone laughed. He saw Ariel's serious expression and stopped.

"You really mean that don't you?"

"Yes. I was never built for this family even though I was born into it. I wanted out with Matthew. It seemed like a real possibility. Who knows, it could be with you too."

"Ariel, this is the only life I've ever known. I don't know how realistic that is."

"Well, let's not think about that today, let's do what the gods put us on the planet to do, while we have time to do it."

She kissed Stone and holstered her gun.

He said, "Let's go put your world right."

He slid out of bed and got dressed. They went to go find justice for Matthew and her unborn child.

Chapter 26

They stood on top of a train trestle, their scope rifles slung across their backs.

Ariel stood silently next to Stone as he looked through the binoculars at their first target. "Set your target."

"When's the next train set to arrive?"

"Don't worry about it. We only have one shot at this. Get on your belly. The door is opening. He's coming out."

Ariel's blood began to pound in her ears. Her hands felt like two blocks of ice. Her mouth was dry. Her skin hot all over. Lowering herself to the tracks she lined up Scott in the site of the rifle scope.

"Now," Stone commanded.

She hesitated for a second. The image of Matthew dying in her arms invaded all of her senses.

She squeezed the trigger. Brain matter exploded and Scott crumpled to the ground. The tracks began to vibrate and Stone lifted her to her feet by her shirt collar.

"Run!"

Memories of Matthew cascaded like a waterfall through Ariel's mind as they fled through the subway with their guns across their back. Their first night in the music room. Making love on the sheet music. Writing the Broadway show. Their magical honeymoon. Their magical time together done.

All slipping into a chamber of her heart. She locked those memories in that chamber and locked them away forever.

As chaos ensued; Ariel froze. She watched Kate hover around her nephew. For the briefest of moments she felt a wave of guilt. Tears threatened to fall down her cheeks.

She looked up at Stone. She seemed to be asking, what do I do with this? He swept her up in his arms and he raced them to safety where they would not be discovered.

ADRIANA LET HERSELF into her flat. She took off her scarf and kicked off her boots. She walked into the bathroom and pulled off her shirt and washed her face. She brushed her teeth. She figured she would finally get a good night's sleep. Frankie was good for that. He didn't have any notions of a love affair and neither did she. Just a good time when Beale reminded her that once upon a time she had dreamed of a future with him.

That once she dreamed of ruling her father's empire alongside him. She opened the medicine cabinet and reached for a bottle of Ambien. Hopefully, the vivid dreams will not come this time.

Adriana poured two or three pills into her hand and dry swallowed them. Then placed the bottle back in the medicine chest. She closed the medicine cabinet. Splashed her face when she came up for air Leo Spencer was there.

"Belle, it's been a long time."

Whirling around grabbing a razor.

"Get out of here you sick sonofabitch."

"Now is that anyway to talk to your hero?"

"You're not my fucking hero! Now leave before I cut you from stem to stern."

"Such bold words from such a scared little girl."

He grabbed her by her hair and slammed her to the ground, "You set my nephew up. Now I'm going to teach what a real man is like in the sack."

Adriana roared in anger and Leo smashed a vase over her head.

"Sorry Belle, but almost dead sex is the best kind."

He whipped off his belt and wrapped it around her neck and began to brutally rape her.

STONE PUSHED ARIEL against the shower wall. He knew it was against all common sense. He loved her. He would always love her. Even if he was just a conduit for her to forget. He thrust inside of her and came. And though he would never admit it. He wanted a family with her. He prayed against all the odds that he would get it.